The
Tragedy
of
Tenaya

A Yosemite Indian Story

By Allan Shields
Illustrated by Richard M. Shields

Published by the Jerseydale Ranch Press, 1992,

 Jerseydale Ranch
6506 Jerseydale Road
Mariposa, California 95338
(209) 742-7972

All drawings and photographs by Richard M.
Shields with the exception of two drawings:
Mt. Hemlock on page 44, and Cony on page
52, by Will Neely, courtesy of the Yosemite
Research Library, Yosemite National Park, CA.

ISBN 1-882803-01-9

Library of Congress Catalog Card Number
92-97499

(A) blindness in human beings...is the blindness with which we all are afflicted in regard to the feelings of creatures and people different from ourselves.

We are practical beings, each of us with limited functions and duties to perform. Each is bound to feel intensely the importance of his own duties and the significance of the situations that call these forth. But this feeling is in each of us a vital secret, for sympathy with which we vainly look to others. The others are too much absorbed in their own vital secrets to take an interest in ours. Hence, the stupidity and injustice of our opinions, so far as they deal with the significance of alien lives. Hence, the falsity of our judgments, so far as they presume to decide in an absolute way on the value of other persons' conditions or ideals.

William James
On a Certain Blindness in Human Beings

Contents

I	The Generous Mountains	1
II	Grizzly	6
III	Sierran Winter	11
IV	Tenaya the Chief	15
V	Loiya	19
VI	The Invaders Come	23
VII	Over the Sierra to Mono	29
VIII	Tenaya's Pride	33
IX	Earth Danger	37
X	Emissary to the Chowchillas	40
XI	Major Savage	45
XII	The Invaders in The Valley	50
XIII	Spring in Ahwahnee	53
XIV	Indignity and Assault	57
XV	The Descent from Above	59
XVI	The Battle at Lake Pyweack	61
XVII	Capture and Resignation	65
XVIII	Promises and Defaults	69
XIX	Tenaya's Hegira	71
XX	The Game of Death	77
Epilogue		81
Author's Note		83

Chapter I
The Generous Mountains

The game started.

Tenaya sat on the ground flanked by two other men of the Ahwahneechees. Chief Kuna of the Monos sat opposite them with two younger men who had helped carry Pinyon nuts and Kachavee fly larva across the Sierra from Mono Lake to Ahwahnee to trade. Early summer followed a mild winter and spring. Mono Pass, though not clear of snow, could be crossed with little difficulty. The winter separation of the old friends heightened the warmth of their meeting. The game was a friendly one.

Kuna and his men had a Rabbit skin blanket spread across their knees, while Tenaya and his partners used a skin blanket of the Black Bear. Each team held four Deer shank bones, two of them with a fern root tied around, and two plain ones. The bones were passed beneath the blanket from hand to hand. The opposing players guessed which hands held the bones. If they guessed that one person held both marked bones one man would snap out two fingers at him and say "Tep!" If plain, he said, "Wi!" The penalty for a wrong guess, like the reward of winning, varied. Guessing both bones correctly brought highest winnings.

This game was among friends. Tenaya had been raised among the Monos at the Lake. His mother was a Mono, his father an Ahwahneechee. Tenaya's father and the remnants of the tribe who had been living in Yosemite Valley and vicinity had been forced by the black sickness and starvation to leave. When Tenaya became a young man, a wise one among the Ahwahneechees told him of the Ahwahnee Valley and its wealth of acorns, deep Kisskisska grasses that are ideal for baskets, of its sky-high walls of grey rock, and of its fish-full rivers and streams. The grey head spoke of the game, the plenty of the region below the valley where winters could be spent. Above all he spoke fervently to Tenaya of the pride in the strength and skills of the Ahwahneechees who were now scattered among various villages. He could find a few here and there, bring them back and could raise up The People to be a strong tribe once again. This was many winters ago.

Though the game tonight was friendly, the stakes were placed high enough to strike interest. Since the Pinyon crop last fall was large Kuna felt safe in placing quite a lot of the carry in the wager against acorns that did not occur on the eastern side of the Sierra in Mono Basin. With luck he could double the amount of acorns, a favorite food. After side bets were placed by onlookers, Tenaya's team began passing the bones.

Kuna and his men were noisy players. They believed that the advantage of detection of the subtle muscular changes in the eyes and faces of opposing players lay with those making disturbing noises, shouting, singing and clapping hands. Loud laughter was another trick. On the other hand, when their own moves were being guessed, noise making helped to conceal tiny clues of expressions of awareness they might show. They therefore made lots of noise to try to elicit clues from the other team and to hide their own.

Tenaya and his men were quiet players. Imperturbability, a silent sameness no matter how exciting the stakes, produced the best tricks of wits. Whether on defense or challenge one could out-play by keeping one's countenance inscrutable. It had a further advantage of unsettling more volatile and mercurial players. After a few hours of saying almost nothing, talkative, flamboyant teams began to get more excitable and unguarded in their actions. Under such circumstances, with rich stakes, feelings sometimes ran high.

This was a game of wits, intelligence, and strength of

personality. Though a gambling game, it was friendly. Though exciting, it was a game played in peace, amid peaceful surroundings. The earth was good to The People.

Ahwahnee was warm during the day this time of year, but nights were still cold. Tenaya and his village therefore chose to live at the Rock Caves near the lake of reflections. The Rock Caves were higher than the surrounding valley floor. Tenaya knew that cold air follows the water courses. To be warmer at night they slept up on the slopes. To avoid the nightly downdrafts they positioned themselves to keep winds at their feet. Simple adjustment to natural conditions was a way of life for The People.

Understanding what plants were good to eat, what were good for illness and what were poisonous; understanding where deer feed, how to spear a rabbit in its burrow with a stick, or stun fish with the fluid of soaproot, buckeye, or squirting cucumber---such insights had come only slowly to them. They had learned from The People in Mexico, in Utah, and in Oregon through indirect and direct contact. From time back out of memory and time beyond campfire stories they had learned to understand the ways of the land.

The People knew how to remove the bitterness from the acorn of the bountiful oaks and to use the mash in many forms. They knew Black Widow Spider and Rattlesnake. Deadly Nightshade and Mushrooms were known. Tenaya's people knew infections and death in childbirth. Racking sorrow and passional love they knew.

Best of all the Ahwahneechees loved the land. How good it was to browse with friends and family in the meadows of tender grasses and clovers in early summer. The young men especially often returned elated from their hunting trips out of the valley to the high country. Spirits seemed to rise with physical elevation until the moment when they were on some mountain summit to ambush Mountain Sheep or Deer. Exhilaration then was theirs and some of it could be shared.

These men were skilled mountaineers. Experience had

taught them how to use their bare feet to cling to steep slopes with the flat, when to expect and use feldspar knobs sticking out from the granite surface. They had learned direct routes up the cliffs, which were passable in high water, and which in snow. They were able to travel rapidly when necessary, and even at night. Courageous and skillful though they were, they avoided the Grizzly Bear and were fearful.

The older men often accompanied the young on the hunting trips, for one of their responsibilities was to carry in the game. Since they were less fleet than the young, it was a fair division of labor. Nor was all the game a burdensome Buck Deer. A few Sooty Grouse from the sunny back slope of Pyweack Peak, two Snowshoe Hares from Tuolumne Meadows, or perhaps a succulent fawn from the Morraine Meadow at White Wolf. Then, too, the older men would tell the stories of hunting prowess, of dangers narrowly averted, and sometimes of the death of a young hunter from a rock fall.

After a long high trip for game, it was good to reach the elevated cliff-top of Ahwahnee, to stop and rest before descending three-thousand feet on the trail. It was good to return to the company of friends and family in the village, to enter the sweathouse and hear the gossip and bragging, then to rush out to the cleansing river and plunge in as they had done before the hunt. Later at night, just before going to sleep, the tired hunters and their companions might enjoy puffing a pipe of native tobacco, strong enough to induce sleep if the strenuous work of the hunting trip were not alone sufficient.

It was late when the game was stopped. Neither side lost or gained much in the wagering. All had gained in enjoyment and companionship. One of Kuna's young men asked Tenaya if he had seen the small group of strange men that had traveled in their direction up Red Rock Canyon in early spring. No, he had not, but one of his hunters reported sighting some strange people looking into the valley, and later found their tracks. They had moved on.

As Tenaya pulled the skin blanket over himself he was

vaguely troubled again by the report of strangers on the land. It was not the first such occasion.

Summer was here. The dry night air was redolent of pine pollen and cedar oil. The odors of The People near were comforting. Hutulu, the Horned Owl hooted. Sounds of sleeping family and friends, mere forest murmurs, lulled him. Then he remembered his combat with the Grizzly years ago and the naming of his People.

Chapter II
Grizzly

It was not difficult to recall his encounter with the most fearsome beast of the Sierra forests. The combat was his most terrifying experience. No doubt he would not have survived his wounds or saved himself had he not been a strong young man of twenty. Then, too, there was the dog.

Not many months after Tenaya and the regathered Ahwahneechees returned to Ahwahnee, Tenaya walked up the valley from the little village in the meadow near Yosemite Falls. He had been learning about their territory piece by piece, so that he would have first-hand, intimate knowledge in case he should ever need it. Acknowledged chief of the Ahwahneechees, he was too young and too untried to be accepted as a leader yet.

As he walked toward the waters of reflection he noticed that there were more very large boulders the closer he got to Tysiack, the huge rock dome with one-half missing. This would be an excellent place for retreat, he thought, in case of an attack on his People. Besides the great boulders for conceal-ment there is water, fuel for warmth, and ample high places nearby for lookouts and defense positions.

He walked on, barely noticing the small dog who tagged along with him. Kept mainly for food, it happened that occasionally one animal would become a pet. Ky had selected Tenaya to follow for some time, even though Tenaya was not given to demonstration of affection, and only rarely acknowl-edged the dog's presence with food.

His walk carried him a couple of miles up Pyweack Canyon before he realized he had gone so far. It was early evening and he had told his old friend that they would talk together at campfire. He turned back.

On reaching the waters of reflection he stopped to watch the changing image on the surface, and wondered about the spirit of so huge and massive a rock as the half-dome, with its tear stained face and resolute visage.

As he left the waters and entered the place of boulders he was half dreaming, not watching his trail, when there suddenly loomed a hulking giant of a bear. In the half light the bear, missing the scent, was also startled by the sudden presence of man and he momentarily stopped. In that instant Tenaya, snapped to emergency wit, decided he could not run and escape the lightning charge of the Grizzly. He was much too close for that. In a distance race he could easily wind the beast. But for a quick start few animals are more swift of foot or more powerful. There was no retreat, no hiding place.

Tenaya had met Grizzly rarely, but had learned a great deal from others. Given warning he will raise himself to get the advantage of sight and smell. He will charge unprovoked, or he will simply stand his ground. If attacked he will raise himself--or he may not. All of this and more, Tenaya recalled in a flash.

Tenaya seized a dead stump of a small cedar with its tough, sharp root intact, that lay at his feet. Unexpectedly, he approached the animal. His stealthy, wary steps left no doubt with the bear that he meant to attack. Grizzly at once raised himself, Tenaya jumped forward, forcing Grizzly to counterattack. As the bear came down, Tenaya stepped to one side and gave a mighty swing with the stump, striking Grizzly's head and dazing him, drawing blood.

Hurt and enraged, the beast sprang round and was about to crush Tenaya by sheer massive bulk when the small dog raced from behind and sank his teeth into his leg. With a swipe of his forepaw, Grizzly flicked Ky over his shoulder and into the top of a manzanita bush where the wind was knocked out of him. Tenaya was able to get in another head blow, this time breaking the lower jaw. Now wounded and crazed, the great bear stumbled as he charged. As he jumped to one side of the charge, Tenaya struck another powerful blow on the top of the head. Grizzly, snarling and screaming, closed for the kill, seized Tenaya with his front legs and dropped dead. Tenaya lost consciousness.

Night had fallen when Tenaya awoke from his dream, except that it was no dream. There he lay in the powerful arms of the Grizzly, mightiest of the First People. Nearby lay the small dog, his left front leg gashed and bleeding. Ky whined and licked Tenaya's hand. Looking down, Tenaya beheld a long, deep gash in his belly. In falling, his head had hit a rock and blood was oozing from a scalp wound. He fainted once more.

Dawn comes slowly to Ahwahnee. Sunlight comes fast. Sun himself revived Tenaya. Pulling himself out from the Grizzly's forepart at great cost of energy, he tried to walk. He lacked the strength for it. He recalled the legend of Tootockan-oolah and how the little measuring worm inched his way from the bottom to the very top of El Capitan to rescue Bear Cubs.

Tenaya crawled slowly along the trail in the direction of the village, resting every few feet, and Ky limped slowly along with him. Soon they came to water where both man and dog drank deeply. Somewhat refreshed, they began their pain-filled trip to the village.

Loiya found him unconscious with knees and hands bleeding and his great wound weakening him. He had gotten to within a quarter of a mile of the village. With the help of others he was carried in. One of the children carried Ky.

Not until the following morning did Tenaya stir and only then did he take more water. Loiya cared for him possessively, seeming to feel that he was somehow her special prize, for she did find him and cared for him out there in the wild, did she not? And was she not young, strong and wild herself?

The story of Tenaya's great combat was told over and over again in every village for many months. No one forgot to name Ky and to wonder at his small dog courage.

Some of The People in other villages were moved to dream of the incident, considered to be a particularly portentous sign, and some were moved to eloquent and fervent speech in order to convey the fuller, awesome meanings to the young. And some made song-speech about the young chief of the Ahwahneechee People with the new name: the Yosemitees.

Chapter III
Sierran Winter

In the Sierra the winters run to extremes. Any one week, indeed any one day, can see violent storms change to a quiet, spring-like warmth. Though the air may be cold at the higher elevations, the sun's radiant energy warms.

With the coming of winter storms Tenaya and his band would move west down the Merced River Canyon, often staying just below the valley a few miles near El Portal. Sometimes they would descend even farther to some sunny open spot along the South Fork of the Merced River such as Hite's Cove, or they could find comfort during mild winters at Kisskisska Meadow, a little lower than their loved valley, but removed from the high areas of heavy snows and lower temperatures.

Not that they were forced to leave, not always. The Caves could be made warm, and the sweathouses, dome-shaped, mud-covered and wind-proof, were ample protection against the storms' winds and cold. Even their wickiups, Cedar bark covered teepee-shaped dwellings, could be made comfortable, if the weather were not severe. The People had learned to build small fires to keep them warm, not large fires to drive them back to the cold air. Still, at Kisskisska Meadow they could live in the meadow borders among the Black Oaks, hunt in the Sugar Pine, Ponderosa Pine, Fir and Cedar forests where trees soar over one hundred and fifty feet into the clear, dry Sierra light.

Kisskisska Meadow was a preferred winter village site for a different reason. It most nearly resembled their valley home, and without the rigors. If snow came, it seldom piled high or lasted long. Freezing temperatures sometimes kept the smoke curling out of the wickiups night and day. Then the sun and warmth brought the inhabitants out again into the open world.

Though the Ahwahneechees never practiced agriculture by cultivating crops, nor domesticated animals, unless one counts dogs as food, they had learned to store acorns in their chuckahs built off the ground of limbs and parts of cedars and ceanothus bushes, bound together with wild grape vines. These large, woven storage places were able to shed water and were, to some extent, rodent proof. In any event, these made it possible to remain in the valley on occasion long after the acorn crop had dropped in the fall.

There were many other food resources, even in the winter, to sustain them. Some deer remained. Rabbits, birds, and fish were plentiful if the winter were not bitter. And the seeds of grasses, nuts of the Pinyon pine, dried meat, and stored plant bulbs assured them ample food for winter when they chose to remain.

The People were wild and lived with wildness.

Other wild creatures also chose to descend during the coldest months. Most birds come down from the higher elevations at Tuolumne Meadows, or from up on the mountain summits. But Sierra Nevada Rosy Finch stays up all winter long at the very summits, only dropping over to the lee sides of the mountains' tops when the most violent wintry blasts drive them to it. Sooty Grouse stays up all winter, eating the tender end needles of the pines. On the ground under where they have perched you can find the tiny pressed logs of their droppings as evidence. Deer annually descend by ancient routes convenient for ambush by Mountain Coyote, Mountain Lion and The People alike. Mountain Sheep descend to the east side for the most part, deer to the west. Black Bear goes down part way, too. The very vegetation including trees could be said to limit its movement up and down the mountains by climate conditions, only its shifts are much slower. Fish did not occur at the higher lakes and rivers and streams, such as in Tuolumne, for the towering glaciers of the ice age had scoured them all out and forced them to live only at lower places. Their return back up to high lakes was much slower because largely accidental, by eagles dropping live ones, and artificial, carried in by man.

The wild creatures, given the choice, descend to milder conditions of life only when necessary. Without realization or having any forethought they simply pursue the easier conditions of life for a few months. Mountain dwellers can never go very far down from their homes, though, so you rarely find them, any of them, moving farther down than they need to go. Never to the lower San Joaquin Valley itself. This is true of animals, plants, trees, and the Ahwahneechees.

Chapter IV
Tenaya the Chief

Through his period of recovery from the fight with the Grizzly, Loiya cared for Tenaya, and their bonds of affection multiplied and grew strong.

Loiya came with her family from the western slope along the Tuolumne River, from a village below Hatchatchie. Though her family stemmed from the Ahwahnee tribe they had since intermarried with the Miwok tribes from the northern section. As a result her skin color was a darker brown than Tenaya's. Both possessed very dark eyes, generous mouths without thick lips, and broad noses. Their long black hair was fine and they kept it neatly combed and brushed, gathered behind the head and allowed to hang to the waist, men and women alike. The winter following his injuries was spent at Kisskisska Meadow above the South Fork of the Merced River. By early spring Tenaya was in full strength and well mended. When the new reddish leaves of the Oaks appeared, Tenaya gathered his dentalium shell money and walked over to Loiya's family wickiup to speak to her father.

The time had long passed when the young chief would normally have arranged for a wife. The problems of gathering The People exploring the territory, and establishing the villages had occupied his time. Since a wife would be a help in a number of ways, it was important for him to have one. At least one. She would be a household help, of course. Beyond that a wife was a sign that the man would stay with the village for life. It was a sign of loyalty and commitment. Taking a wife was a sign of willingness to assume mature responsibilities, including those involving children. Occasionally, when a man could make reasonable use of more, it was important for the village welfare for him to take more than one wife. Though

15

there was no especial favoritism attached to any one, the first one was considered to be the focus of family life.

Tenaya approached the father, spoke of his desire for Loiya to be his wife and offered three arms of dentalium money. The father countered that she was worth more, for she was healthy, strong, and had already demonstrated how she would care for the young chief in times of need. He proposed that Tenaya add to the cost a long obsidian glass blade valued for its workmanship and meaning, not for its use, and that he include his collection of Porcupine quills and Red Shafted Flicker feathers.

Tenaya agreed to the price but asked to withhold some of the Flicker feathers. With the arrangement thus completed, Loiya, who had been off a short distance pretending not to hear, was called by her father to come. He told her briefly what Tenaya had done. She smiled and walked away with Tenaya. The marriage was complete.

The father watched the two young people walk away quickly in the direction of Tenaya's wikiup, their firm bodies glistening in the warm sun, their long black hair moving from side to side on their backs. The father turned to see his third wife bringing watercress greens up from Skelton Creek.....

Tenaya's abilities as a chief soon became clear to all in the village and beyond. Young in years he was old in intelligence. He had the wit to consult with age before deciding issues within the band. His approach to the hand gambling game, of the quiet, keen observer being a good shepherd to his own thoughts, and then deciding forcefully, carried over into his other judgments. Even while hunting, the men noticed, he rarely made a quick decision but that when he did decide it was a good one. Soon they consulted with him, young and old alike.

His value in dealing with the Monos was especially important in establishing him as chief in fact as well as in name. As part Mono, he was accepted by them and they were glad to deal with Tenaya and gave him fair shares. Often they would cooperate in hunts in the high regions for Mountain Sheep and Deer where no tribal territories were ever established.

Then, too, Tenaya was respected by the Chowchilla People in Coyote territory on the upper South Fork of the Merced River. Aggressive and quick to anger with those they did not like or trust, they were reassured, and friendly with Tenaya and the Yosemites, as they came to call them. For they had heard of the unbelievable combat with the Grizzly.

Tenaya could be tender and kindly with his People. When trouble arose he patiently searched out the words of all concerned and never decided before doing so. In this way he won respect even from those who could not always accept his decision.

It was not apparent until you knew him for a long time that Tenaya was part poet and dreamer. At times he could become as eloquent as the Elderberry Bush, the source of all music. During the ceremony of the Cry for a dead member, it was Tenaya they turned to for the first talk and song. Near the end of the fifth day, it was Tenaya again, brought in his ecstatic dream state to sing and to speak of the dead and the land of Elowin in the west waters of Ocean. Whenever a spokesman was sought by visiting People or by runners from neighboring villages, Tenaya was chosen.

At the times of annual feast when several villages got together for celebration, members of other bands would seek out this man to discuss their particular problems, matters of territorial dispute, food shortages, wrong marriages, banishments, and similar difficulties.

In this manner Tenaya, starting as a young chief of a new village, grew up with his village's reputation and waxed strong in himself. At the base of his reputation stood the Grizzly.

All of The People knew that Grizzly was the fiercest and most evil of The First People, that his flesh should never be eaten for its spiritual content was wrong, made up of the worst of human deeds. Hunters knew how often Grizzly cut down young children who had wandered too far from the village, and old men out on a hunt, up and down the land. Hunters knew that it was useless to fight Grizzly with small spears, bows and arrows, and rocks. Hunters knew only one way of handling Grizzly--flight.

Thus the news of Tenaya's achievement spread through the land an immediate respect for his courage, strength, and prowess on the kill. What he did with Grizzly was only a suggestion of what he could do with lesser game, such as man. Then too Tenaya was spiritually to be set above the Wise Ones, even above the Shamans, for he had passed into the land of Elowin in the western waters of death and had returned to life, bringing back skills and knowledge possessed by no one who has not himself had such experiences.

By his personal achievements and qualities of character Tenaya raised the respect and admiration for his Yosemitees in the eyes of all. Tenaya became their chief.

Chapter V
Loiya

In the years following their marriage Loiya proved to be a valuable wife and mother of three sons, of whom Tenaya was profoundly proud. Since her upbringing took place on the western side of the Sierra she was well acquainted with the plants and animals, how to prepare them most tastefully, and what rare treats to watch for. In these matters she was a constant help to the young women of the village who had come from the east side, or who simply had to be taught to become women of the tribe. For their responsibilities were many, and the traditions strong.

Like her husband, Loiya was robust of physique and steady in her personality. Some might call her stolid or taciturn but they would be those who had not been an acquaintance for very long. After fifteen or twenty years of close association in a small village, every person becomes intimately and deeply related to everyone. The merest glance of intent can be read--and misread--by such associates. Controls were strict. Justice was swift and sometimes seemingly harsh to an outsider who might fail to detect the subtleties of such interpersonal relations. And Loiya was mistress of the tribe. Not a little of the strength of the Yosemitees had its source in her influence on The People.

Loiya's skill in gathering rare items was great. She knew where to look for San Diego Towhee and to bring in his special russet feathers and the white side tail feathers that formed an undergarment as he flew. She knew of a small patch of the prized Pinyon Pine, rare on the western slope, near Hatchatchie in Tiltill Valley on Rancheria Creek and would connive to send special hunters there for her in late summer and fall to gather nuts. Since this was beyond their territory there were risks involved.

Loiya even had a way of fixing Kit-kit-dizze into a tea that was especially good and warming on winter evenings.

She taught the girls to gather milkweed and to make a string with it, to shred dogbane fibers and bark of old cedar trees, to make a moccasin with only two parts to stitch together, and to make fire with buckeye wood. Though the men took care to instruct the boys in hunting, defense, and attack, still Loiya, like many a mother, took special pains to see that her sons knew the traditions and land.

Gathering the seed of grasses required a precise sweeping motion with the basket, and an understanding of when to take them. Fern tops, of the bracken, picked when just unfolding, were a special treat that was seasonal. Their nutty flavor was a prized addition to the regular larder.

Loiya discovered a better way to catch insects, particularly the grasshopper. Instead of using the old way of driving them towards a fire pit from two sides by lines of women and girls, she designed a long trench in which the top was narrower than the bottom. In this way the grasshoppers were not scorched and lost but could be gathered and roasted with more control. Not all soil worked with this method but the soils of both Ahwahnee and Kisskisska Meadow did.

Sometimes the entire village worked together in gathering food and game, carrying in any especially large catches. When the water was low they would work together to stun and collect trout in the river, for there were many fish to collect once the soaproot milk mixed with sand and water was added to the river. Gathering of fuel was another task that could be shared. All were kept busy and in remarkable ways may be said to have shared a kind of contentment. They knew how to accept their conditions with grace and dignity....

One day early in 1850 Loiya was gathering some buckeye wood near El Portal when a young hunter came running by, breathless from his exertions. She stopped him and asked to know why he was in such flight. He told her that strange men had been waiting for them to come along on their usual trail looking for deer, and had killed his two friends without any cause or reason. It was as though they were the game the strangers were hunting.

Loiya herself carried the news to Tenaya at once.

Chapter VI
The Invaders Come

The news of the killings disturbed Tenaya and the entire village. Two of the strongest hunters, young but wise in the ways of the natural world, had been cut down by the strangers near Savage's new trading post. This was a great loss for the small community to suffer.

Tenaya performed his first duties, ordering ten men to bring in the bodies for cremation, and starting the preparations for the Cry Ceremony that would last for five days and nights continuously. They believed that The People were born immortal but could be deprived of it by accident, wrong deeds, or some evil. Celebrations by the living were the best chance for the departed spirit to escape into Elowin. Runners were dispatched to neighboring villages with strings of milkweed tied with the number of knots until the day the Cry would begin. One knot was to be untied each day.

The People had known for many years of the coming of the strangers from beyond the frame of the world to settle. Even as a child Tenaya had seen the light men in Mono country. One of his friends, an older boy, had tried to rub off the white color to find the true brown beneath and could not. The white strangers were friendly, all smiles and gifts, and left The People to go their own way, without invading territories.

Tenaya had heard early in his life of the mission fathers, of how they had brought ways of growing food, new ideas and strange stories of a world unseen. He had heard, too, of floggings of The People who disobeyed demands by the white masters. By The People, flogging was considered to be worse than death. No one struck a child, much less another adult being, unless he wished to deliver the worst possible insult and indignity. Fighting itself was uncommon. Physical combat with spears, bows and arrows rarely went beyond the point where one or two persons on a side were injured. War was never entered except for revenge for wrongs committed against the village or against some member of it. Violence was familiar to The People but it was accepted as conduct to be avoided whenever possible.

The missions had brought death to The People. While winning souls, they were losing the individuals, and they saw each day the clear eventual result of their ways of dealing with the natives. New diseases killed, divisions of belief created conflicts. The new destroyed, not assisted, the old. This Tenaya had heard about.

At no time had the Pohonochees, Chowchillas, Monos, or Ahwahneechees been invaded. Recently a James Savage from the Fresno River had established a new trading post at the confluence of the South Fork of the Merced River and the Merced. Though his men had killed and frightened away game, they had not asked for or taken territory. Savage had taken several wives from The People but he had paid well for them. Some thought he had too many, that he used them as servants, not as wives, and they resented the treatment of them.

But these events were removed far enough from Ahwah-nee to be no direct threat to them, except in summer.

Now they had killed. Perhaps they were invaders after all. Was it possible that they had now changed, and would try to take territory from The People? It had happened elsewhere. Would the killing continue? Was this an act declaring their hostility toward The People?

From the upper edge of the world there had come parts of stories, bit by bit. Remote and unreal as they sounded when related, their meaning might after all be clear now. The Invaders had come.

Tenaya and some of the men spoke of these matters at length in the sweathouse for several days, trying to be sure of what it all meant to their future as a village, and of the future of The People. These two stories were related over and over as evidence of what to expect from The Invaders, the Story of Bloody Rock, and The Wiyot Massacre.

Bloody Rock came as the last part of a longer story about The People of Pomo and Chumaia.

The Chumaias' territory had been invaded by miners and others who sold to miners. Some of the miners hired some Chumaia men to work for them and paid them well, but when the miners wanted to start a new mine in Chumaia country The People objected. The miners then moved in by force. With guns and horses the miners were strong. In moving in and forcing their way, they killed some of the Chumaias, who then took revenge by stealing and killing when they could. The People did not like the miners to cut their food crops, kill and frighten their game, and take their land. Then, too, more and more miners came.

The Chumaias counseled with the Pomos that they must defend themselves, kill The Invaders, and drive them from their territory. The Pomos, who had not been invaded, feared battle with the powerful whites with their guns and horses and refused to join the Chumaias. Instead they spoke with the miners and told of the plan.

The Invaders organized at once to stop such actions before they began, equipped and outfitted a company of experienced fighters paid for such work. These men rode into Chumaia villages, burned the dwellings, brained the children against trees, shot women, and cut down the men as they found them, taking scalps, and running riot over the entire area inhabited by Chumaias.

At this point a band of forty Chumaias, mostly women and children, became separated from their fellows and were surrounded by the company of fighters. Crazed with fear, hiding night and day, bone tired, half starved, the band sought refuge on top of a huge boulder that stuck out from the mountain, the top of which could be reached only by a large crack where it joined the mountain. A traditional safe place of retreat under normal combat with arrows and short engagements, it was a trap under these circumstances.

One of The Invaders came to the rock and told them they were doomed. They could stay and starve, stay and be shot, or jump to their death.

There followed a long period of silence and then the Chumaias began their Cry songs. They joined hands and stood together singing, then they parted and danced a long time, chanting and wailing, preparing themselves for the thing to be done. Down below they could see The Invaders on horseback waiting, though they were no longer a threat to them.

Suddenly a signal from one of the men stopped the dance, they rejoined on a line, held hands and still singing walked to the edge and stepped off into space together.

Tenaya had heard this.

He had heard, too, about the Wiyot Massacre. It was impossible to know of the truth of the events, but this he heard.

The Wiyot people celebrate their great feast in midwinter, meeting together on an island in Humboldt Bay called Dulawat, with smaller groups at two other nearby villages. About two hundred and fifty men, women, and children gather together to dance, dress, sing and feast, holding their meetings in several huts with a capacity of about fifty persons in each.

The huts were crowded. The People were completely absorbed in the dancing and singing. All were dressed in their most colorful and elaborate costumes. Furs and feathers, leather work and grease paint filled the air with exciting odors and sounds. The shuffling and pounding of feet, the beating of the sacred drums, the monotonous, hypnotizing wails had carried on for two days and nights of the "Ten Nights Dance." Some had taken drugs to heighten the spells. Some were on the verge of the dance madness that seizes those who do not stop to rest or eat once in a while. Each hut, with its small fire providing the only night light, issued smoke from the top of the roof. Each hut was a kind of instrument of music, resounding with the created beats, sighs, and songs of men, women, and children meeting in delirium.

With the bodies moving up and down, swaying from side to side, legs raised and lowered in perfect rhythm, the shadow world on the sides and ceiling of the domed huts became more startlingly real than the contrived and somewhat forced world that produced it.

The night grew long. Fatigue was beginning to show in the actions of the dancers. The spells were seizing a few when it happened.

For a while no one could tell that anything unusual was going on. At first only a few cries of children penetrated the thick wall of ceremony sounds. That was only for a short time. For then agonizing screams broke in upon the cadence of Wiyot life as axe, club, and knife of The Invaders did their deadly work.

Women and men were clubbed and chopped into senselessness. Babies were knifed to death and tossed aside. Methodically, according to a well conceived plan worked on long in advance of the act, the white men butchered their ways into the huts, blocking the only exit with grisly guards while the executioners prepared the sacrifices to the golden god.

Dazed, unarmed for the ceremonies, and stupefied by their exertions, The People were utterly at the mercy of the white ones, and they were merciless and thorough.

Perhaps six escaped. Three old men were knifed and played dead until morning, and three or four guards swam for the mainland. Only two Invaders were killed. They had disguised themselves as The People to gain the advantage and were decapitated by their fellows.

The next morning the tide ran red with the blood of more than two hundred men, women, and children. Those who escaped reported that The Invaders, unsatisfied with their labors at Dulawat, had gone on to the villages of Witki and Kotsir where their results were even more complete.

This, too, Tenaya had heard.

27

Chapter VII
Over the Sierra to Mono

Tenaya needed more information before deciding what action to take, if any. Some impetuous ones wanted immediate revenge for the killings. Soon those from neighboring villages would arrive with complete news of events in their territories. He wondered about the eastern slope and his Mono friends. Did they know anything that would help him to decide? So many white men were in some far places, he had heard, that you could see men all day without seeing the same one twice. Were they coming to Ahwahnee?

He spoke with Latta, his eldest son, now a man. The snows lay deep on the high country and it was dangerous to cross the Sierra. Still, there had been few storms, and with the skills of survival and travel in winter Latta had learned there was less risk. Tenaya believed, too, that the Monos should be aware of what was happening to the Yosemitees. A trans-Sierra trip was required. It was decided that Latta would make the trip to consult with Chief Kuna about these urgent matters. He prepared to leave.

Latta took a skin robe, his fire stick of buckeye wood, a sack of nuts, seeds, and acorn cakes, and a quantity of dried deer meat. For hunting he needed only some cord for snares and his bow and arrows. Moccasins were a necessity for rough travel, especially in winter snows and over ice. Finally, he took his snow shoes, woven of deer sinew over willow frames.

Leaving El Portal he took the Big Meadow trail up in the general direction toward Crane Flat for a distance, his choice being to ascend to the high country outside Ahwahnee because of the more gradual climbing. Just below the level of Crane Flat he met the snow. A hard crust enabled him to travel fairly swiftly. His superb, mature physical condition made it possible for him to endure strenuous exertion over long periods. By this time he had arrived in the dense, high, giant forest of Red Fir, Sugar Pine, and Incense Cedar. New growth of these trees and the cover of Dogwood and Ceanothus, to say nothing of occasional stretches of impenetrable Manzanita, stiff, brittle, and unyielding, made it necessary for him to choose his trail with careful forethought.

Keeping his direction of travel due east, he skirted the top of Ahwahnee, descended into Yosemite Creek basin in the early afternoon, and then, as he climbed out of the basin he entered the region of heaviest and deepest snows. A recent storm had left powder snow knee deep so that he was forced to wear the snow shoes, thus slowing his progress somewhat. Nevertheless he reached Pyweack Lake after dark and decided to rest for part of the night on the nearby upper rocky slope.

Latta had made many trips here during the spring and summer months, but very few in winter. The Marmots were gone, and most of the birds, he noticed. Still, in late afternoon Coney, the little rock rabbit, had chattered at him in his squeaky, rock-grating voice from a rock talus slope, so some of the animals were active. While crossing a meadow he remembered seeing Gopher's moves beneath the snow, pushing his excess dirt up into the snow as he continued eating roots. In the spring, Latta knew, he would see these dirt ropes laid out along the top of the sod as the snow melted away.

A vast silence of crackling cold air enveloped him in well earned sleep for a short while, only occasionally disturbed by the necessity to feed the small fire at the front of his rock hollow.

Next morning by starlight he started up the ridge into Tuolumne Meadows. He found Mountain Coyote tracks as he entered the meadows by Pothole Dome, dog-like but webbed between the toes. Mountain Coyote was often mistaken for

Wolf, which never has occurred here, because he is larger, and has a much bushier tail than Valley Coyote. The webbed feet of the large Mountain Coyote, like Latta's snow shoes, enabled Coyote to travel over the snow rapidly to catch game.

Latta reached the Tuolumne River early in the morning. Crossing on the ice, he continued his trip up out of the meadows, over snow-covered glacial moraines, still humped in the snow, past Mammoth Peak, around the base of Kuna Crest, and up the long valley between the great, grey crest and the red slopes of Mt. Dana and Mt. Gibbs, until he had reached Mono Pass itself.

A strong afternoon wind had come up as he approached the pass, so that when he emerged from the Lodgepole Pine forest into Willow thickets and Whitebark Pines of the pass, the sounds of the winds in the pines changed. Here the snows were not deep. The recent fall of new snow made it necessary for him to continue using the snow shoes. At the pass itself he walked over behind a large appressed clump of whitebark pine to rest.

As he looked up to the top of Mt. Gibbs he was greeted by a new sight--snow banners, caused by the new snow being blown off from both sides of the summit but not from the very top where very little snow stays, the two streams of snow meeting on the lee side and then being carried as one off hundreds of feet into the deep blue sky. He looked about and saw that each peak--Mammoth, Dana, Koip--all had white banners streaming out from their summits, like the long white hair of some dream maidens.

Pulling his rabbit skin robe about him more tightly, he began to descend the Red Rock Canyon into Mono basin. He had not gone down more than a mile when he saw an apparition, what he thought at first was an illusion, a mirage. His travel had carried him across so much snow in clear light that he was afraid he was becoming snow-blind, even though he had been careful to shield his head with the robe and to put charcoal black under and about his eyes to absorb some of the glare. There, fifty paces away standing in front of a red rock wall in full view appeared a White Deer. Its antlers, tail, nose and hooves were dark. Its eyes were a deep pink. The lovely beast proudly displayed a magnificent rack of antlers of at least five points and many branched, the weight of them making him keep his neck rigid and head high, adding greatly to his noble appearance.

Small wonder that Latta could scarcely believe his senses momentarily. He had seen a white doe one season, and had seen other white deer skins, but this great specimen would have made the finest robe and false head in the region. It was the prize of a lifetime--and he could not even consider trying to take him alone.

As though the thought had communicated to the buck stag, he turned and bounded off, stiff legged, to the opposite side of the canyon, down into willow thickets and was lost to Latta's fixed and admiring gaze. What a vision he would have to relate to the Monos that very night and later, on his return, to the men and boys in his own sweat-house in Ahwahnee!

Soon Latta was down out of the snow and winds, onto the warmer, sloping plain of the Mono Lake basin, across to the volcanic cones and in camp with his friends with whom he spent the next two days, seeking any information he could ferret out.

No, they had not heard anything recently, nor had they been invaded. No, they had not been across the Sierra, nor gotten word from there, since last fall. There had been some white travelers go through, but like the others, they had gone on north or south and had given them no trouble. Kuna was sufficiently impressed with Tenaya's concern, though, that he decided to send two men back with Latta for The Cry and to bring news.

As the three men started back up toward Red Rock Canyon, Latta noticed two piles of the bones of horses or mules. He had already noted that some members of the Mono village wore articles of clothing of the white men.

32

Chapter VIII
Tenaya's Pride

When Latta and his two Mono companions came into the village at El Portal they could see at once that The Cry had been underway for two or more days. From the dress of the women busying themselves preparing large quantities of acorn meal near the river, and from the dress of the occasional men they saw outside the ceremonial building, they could tell that there were members of the villages of the Potoencies, Pohono-chees, Nootchoos, and Chowchillas. There were even a few Chookchancees from the San Joaquin River area. Representatives came from other villages near and far along the western slope. The fact that there were so many there for The Cry for two young hunters indicated that other kinds of troubles were known and needed telling.

Latta carried his news to Tenaya during one of his periods of rest. As the chief of the village of the victims, it fell to him to be the head of the ceremonies. These duties were arduous and lasted over a very long period of time, four to five days and nights, without long periods of rest.

Tenaya accepted the news and welcomed his son back. He was troubled by the news of the fresh bones of horses and of the articles of clothing the Monos wore but said little to Latta.

As he walked back to the ceremony, regaled in his feather finery made of Red Shafted Flicker, Robin, Red-Winged Blackbird, and Woodpecker for the places where Fire had touched them, he thought of his sons, of how one of them, possibly Latta, would become chief if he were to be replaced.

He thought of their early years and wondered if they had been well prepared for the responsibilities. Especially he thought of the youngest boy, Seethkil, who was even now only a little more than a boy, coming fifteen years later than the second son, Till.

Seethkil had been a very active baby, even in the mother, and was still constantly moving. Unlike his father, he was full of fun and tricks--though never malicious. Instead of making fire, he preferred taking it from a neighbor. He enjoyed trapping Mouse and taming him, taking keen delight in the colors of the fur and in Mouse's lightning actions. It was no accident altogether that Mouse was called the Flute Player by all The People, for Seethkil, catching the spirit from Mouse perhaps, carried his emotional exuberance over into his own music and was considered to be the finest flutist in the village. His sound was distinctive. Not a bright, reedy one the Elderberry sticks often produced with other players, Seethkil's was a soft, mellow, haunting and floating sound that lay easy on the ear, like a rabbit pelt.

At play his energies led him to excel the lazier ones. His aim with arrow and spear alike was true. The spear seemed to come from him as a part of his person, and the strong, direct flight of his arrow began when he reached for the shaft to nock it. Such skill with weapons might easily save his life in fair combat. At Shinny he was quick and sure, slippery as an eel escaping from the wrestling holds, hitting the leather ball the length of the field at times, and always with control. Only in gambling did he have bad luck. Still, he took even chance losses gracefully and cheerfully.

Till, the middle son, was a man now and had shown a strong interest in The People and in their languages, taking great pains to learn new words whenever villages came together for feasts. Till went off of his hunting trails at times to visit in other villages for this purpose. Then too there were the girls....

Till's build was larger than Seethkil's. His shoulders and

chest were heavy but his legs were trim, maybe from the normal exertions of climbing, the constant walking and running. His ankles were thin, like Tenaya's. It was Till who was often selected to run to neighboring villages with news even now that he was more than thirty years old. He was the strongest, though not the fastest, runner in the village. Not prompt--he was one to dally--he was reliable and accurate in report. Till was handsome and loved others.

Latta was the steady one. First born sons may be favored more constantly and carefully than the others, or so Tenaya thought. He was proud and pleased with his sons and wished for their safe futures....

The news from the northern villages was not detailed but the Wiltucumnees told that many villages had found the miners to be friendly, had engaged their sons in work and paid them well. Some of The People had even moved down to be closer to the mines. There had been some killing, but these had usually been individuals who had been bad, stealing and attacking the miners.

The Chowchillas, Nootchoos, and Phononochees had dire news. Members of their villages had worked but had not been paid. Some families had been forced to move when miners came in and threatened them. It was well known that James Savage had taken wives from the Nootchoos and Pohonochees, but had taken none from the Yosemitees. But the Chowchillas had learned that he had thirty-three of them on the Fresno and on the Merced, all young women, that they were paid for, it was true, but they were slaves, not wives. Such indignity could not be suffered. Though Savage had been good to them, had never been known to hurt any of The People, still the Pohonochees had found out from Savage's wives in just the past few days that the pay Savage gave for gold from The People was tiny while he received great pay for it himself, and he had not labored for it. Savage, too, wanted his women to bring all news of The People to him so that he could bring more miners into the land.

35

The Chowchillas and Pohonochees both believed that Tenaya's hunters had been killed by Savage's men who had gone out "to hunt Indians," as they spoke of it. The Pohonochees, who lived in Ahwahnee at Pohono Creek during the summers, wanted to take revenge at once by taking Savage's women away to the mountains again, and by killing Savage and his men.

Tenaya counseled caution. He was not ready to decide on action about this specific incident. He wanted time to try to get more information, possibly from Savage's Trading Post. Had the Pohonochees talked with Savage's wives? Could the killings have been accidental? Were Tenaya's hunters looking for a horse or a mule when they were caught? If they took revenge at the South Fork post, would other whites come up to fight? How many? To these questions the Pohonochees and Chowchillas gave no answer.

After The Cry the villages returned home. Not many days later Tenaya heard that Savage's Trading Post had been attacked after his wives had left him, much was taken, and one man had been killed. Tenaya learned that the attackers were known to Savage and to all the miners. The attackers, they said, were the Yosemitees.

Chapter IX
Earth Danger

The Yosemitees removed at once to Ahwahnee. Even though it was the end of winter and snow was still on the valley floor, nights bitter cold and days short, still for safety they had to return and stay in the Caves. Carrying as many articles of household need as they could, they left El Portal and returned home to the mountains.

The move was made none too soon, for Till, left to watch for any threat from a ledge above the south side of the river above El Portal, saw eight or nine men on horses and mules ride up as far as they could until they reached the place of great boulders, and turn back. They carried rifles and were very excited.

In winter the men slept with the boys in the sweathouse, the women in wickiups. Since they were occupying the same large caves for warmth, there was more than the usual conversation the next few weeks. The women were greatly concerned for the men and children, for they too had heard of the Wiyots and Chumaias and were fearful.

Loiya had tried to convince the women of the Noot-choos, Pohonochees, and Chowchillas that they should act with the Yosemitees. She had complete faith in Tenaya's words. As she drifted off to sleep there in the Caves, she felt cold deep inside her, not from the chill air, but from the fear for her men.

She had barely fallen asleep when she was brought to complete wakefulness by shouts from outside the caves, though she could not understand. Before she had time to rise she had her question answered for she heard the sounds and felt the earth shaking. All about her the others were rousing and rushing toward the outside.

Beyond the Caves were large boulders where the women ground acorns Loiya first noticed that these massive pieces were fairly dancing a ponderous dance. The trees were alive with wild swishing sounds. Some were toppling, cracking, splitting, and dropping dead limbs. Within moments all of this was drowned out by the uproar from the cliffs that tower over half a mile high. The roar of rock sliding and grinding, great masses falling and jostling was deafening. And the fire! The gigantic shifting sparked off fire. The entire valley was light with the purple, luminous brightness that was without earthly source. At the valley rim Loiya could see pieces of forest topple and flow over the edge to fall into the agitated abyss. On Tysiack the snows were loosened and avalanched. Later they found large sections of the forest wiped out. Down a large swath of slope lay the trees, all neatly placed up and down the slope, felled by the single axe blow of the avalanche.

All of this happened in seconds and the earth stood still. The sounds of falling rock subsided and the purple light became a faint blue glow and went out, except for sparks here and there up and down the cliffs.

Latta's wife hurried up to Loiya asking in a troubled voice if she had been Wadacka, their little girl. Loiya, for answer, ran back into the Caves. A small fire, shaken to new brightness by the quake, showed her the child still lay soundly sleeping. Should she let her stay as she is? Ky lay protectively next to Wadacka. As she asked the question the quake came again and just as violent. Loiya called Ky, picked up Wadacka

-- and at once a rock fell on the spot. With her sweet burden in her arms, she turned to run outside. The entrance was no longer there. Debris smothered the fire. In the blackness she tripped and fell. As she fell forward, something stopped her leg and she went numb.

Seethkil, led by Ky, found her in the first light of the winter dawn. With the light of pitch torches of old dead pine limbs he found an access way into the Caves. Wadacka was unharmed and lay beneath the protective form of Loiya, whose weight kept the girl from moving, while Loiya was pinioned by a large, flat piece of granite that had flaked off. Too heavy to raise by hand, cedar poles were brought and the piece was pried up, releasing Loiya.

Her ankle was crushed. To relieve the pain, the Shaman ordered a ceremony in which he gave her some tanuwish root fluid, and sucking on the ankle, produced pebbles from his mouth to show that the trouble was removed and she would become well.

Loiya herself bound the leg in leather. She carried a stiff limb for the rest of her days. The broken wing of such a fine bird only made her flight irregular, not slow or ugly. She was pleased that it happened as it did.

Ever after that night in the Caves, Loiya and Wadacka were rarely separated. And Wadacka always called Ky to her before sleeping, to take his place of rest beside her.

Chapter X
Emissary to the Chowchillas

Tenaya would have taken Latta with him on such an urgent mission where he had to go in person himself, but since Latta was understood to be the next chief, he decided to leave him. He asked Till and Seethkil to accompany him on his trek to the Chowchillas. Trouble, if it started, could easily start with them. They were known for taking what they wanted or needed. Furtive and secretive, they were not likely to tell a runner what Tenaya needed to learn.

The three snowshoed their way up Pohono trail to Wawona at the South Fork of the Merced River, crossed, and followed Big Creek up over Chowchilla Mountain and down to Nippinawassee where the Chowchillas were spending the winter. Situated just over the hump from Coarse Gold, Nippinawassee was near Savage's Trading Post on the Fresno, as well as near Mt. Bullion, Agua Fria, and Mariposa. It was a good source of information from various quarters.

On entering the meadow land of the Chowchilla village, Tenaya could tell that his trip was not in vain, or so he thought then. An approaching storm caused smoke from the wickiups to curl toward the ground. Low, cold clouds and a winter fog made it necessary to wear skin robes. A light, new snow was already on the ground. Tenaya saw that there were many more dwellings than the Chowchillas alone could occupy, and that there were many women and children, some of them from valley villages. This was bad news. Only during times of fighting did this happen, especially during winter.

Other signs were apparent. Seethkil found tracks of horses and cattle almost at once, Till noticed boxes stacked

40

here and there that could only have come from a trading post, and there was the sound of the fighting chants coming from various dwellings.

The Chowchilla chief, Kieyou, greeted Tenaya warmly, thinking that the Yosemitees had thus answered his call to arms. He was greatly disappointed when Tenaya corrected this impression. The Yosemitees were not on the path of combat with anyone, but had come to learn what had happened at Savage's Trading Post and elsewhere in the land.

Mistaking his question to mean Savage's Fresno post, Kieyou blanched noticeably and Tenaya pressed for more information until the facts came clear.

Even before the Cry at El Portal, Kieyou related, he had tried to organize many villages into a force to fight back the advance of the miners. These men were not stopping at any point of advance up the range as long as they could find gold. They had cut many, many oaks, let their animals eat the seed grasses, frightened the game away, set fires in wrong places at bad times, and failed to pay The People for work.

Kieyou went on. James Savage was the chief of The Invaders, the more dangerous because appearing to be friendly. Even now he had gone to a very large village of white people to get men to come fight. His wives, all young, between ten and twenty-two years, had been sold for the night to miners for their drunken pleasures. Savage took large gold from little payment to his helpers. Savage's posts were meeting places where all miners went. They all consulted with him about "the dirty indians," and acted always as though he were chief. He had all their stores of food and clothing, too.

Kieyou's plan was to kill Savage and remove the main strength of the miners. The claims of The People went un- heard. The only Invaders you could trust were dead ones. A band of Chowchillas, Pohonochees, and Noochoos had therefore attacked his South Fork post, but Savage was not there. So a larger band attacked the Fresno post, stripped the goods, killed three men, and drove the animals to the mountains. It was here that they learned of Savage's trip away for more men.

Savage's wives had told of his plan to the Chowchillas when they were safe. A number of them had returned to the villages and had brought other news of the plans of The Invader.

They taught that men in far places had been taking The People to places in the great valley where they were given clothing, food, and material for shelter, strong drink in quantity, and promises for gifts if they would stay. Many of the chiefs had agreed and already had taken their villages down, principally in the northern sections. Those who refused to go were forced to go anyhow.

Thus, Kieyou argued, the only action left was to fight these men by gathering their strength together. If they did not, they too would be forced to go and live in the valley on the reservation.

Tenaya was stunned by all of these matters coming at once and very troubled and confused. He was thinking of his small band of Yosemitees and wondering how all of this affected them.

Were these things true, as Kieyou said them? He spoke with other chiefs in the camp and found that they said the same. If they did not fight, they would be taken.

But if it were true that The Invaders could be so strong on horse- back with rifles, and that there were many, many more who could come, what could such a small group such as these do to fight them off? If they simply agreed and went in, wouldn't that at least let them continue to live in peace? Should they not stay in peace and go farther up into the mountains, or even remove to Mono basin? How could he explain to Kieyou and the others if the Grizzlies, the fiercest of all, should refuse to fight?

Tenaya remembered the Wiyots and Chumaias and spoke at length with Kieyou of all these matters. Especially he remembered the Chumaias, and how they became trapped by the new enemy when they used old ways. He remembered the Wiyots, that The Invaders did not trouble to tell any difference between good and bad men, good and bad deeds.

Would the Yosemitees be the same as all other villages to The Invaders? What would Kieyou do if they did not join?

Even though a driving storm had begun, Tenaya, Till and Seethkil started back over Chowchilla Mountain for their Ahwahnee home. Their hearts were greatly troubled. In their bellies were lead pieces.

Chapter XI
Major Savage

James Savage was known to Tenaya. Savage did not like him or the Yosemitees. The Yosemitees alone would not trade with him. The Yosemitees alone would sell him no wives. Savage could not trust them, which meant that the Yosemitees would not do what he wanted them to do.

When Tenaya found out what Savage wanted he was not troubled. His men were happy in Ahwahnee. They did not need gold, or strange food, or strong drink. Savage could keep his civilized trinkets of amusements. The Yosemitees already possessed what Savage could never know.

The news from Kieyou and the others about Savage getting still more men, of the wives leaving him, of his removing his post from the South Fork of the Merced--all of these things were disturbing.

That Savage had actually gone to the large, far village called San Francisco was true, for he took one of his wives and one of The People of the great valley so that they could bring the news that it was useless for The People to hold out, and that they should accept the generous invitation of the United States Government to come and be wards on the reservations kindly set aside for them to be all together.

On his return, Savage made talks with some of the villagers on the Fresno to try to warn The People that if they did not come in willingly that they would be forced to come in or be driven out and killed. He told of an endless river of men who would come, all with rifles and horses and mules to bring the land to The Invaders, who now had claims on it. The advance of civilized men could not be more than delayed by refusing to come--it could not be stopped. The "Indians" must be brought to see this. The land was not theirs.

Savage was a wealthy man. For one so young, in his twenties, he had done very well in business since coming to the mines. In little more than four years he had learned the languages of the villages of Miwok near Merced and Fresno Rivers, had established a reputation for giving excellent service for a high price, and had so picked his places and wares that he had a virtual monopoly for supplying the miners with necessities, preferring to let the miners dig the gold and taking it in the form of trade. Nor were there real objections from the miners themselves. For Savage saved them the time and energy of traveling the longer distance to the village at Mariposa to pay about the same prices.

By using hired help, and indentured servants, he had a number of sidelines going, mining itself being the most lucrative. With the events of settlement in his favor, he had ambitious plans for expansion of his interests. He was not one to let the natives--even native Americans--thwart him.

The People understood how it was to the advantage of The Invaders--all of them--to have all obstacles to quick acquisition removed. They understood how Savage would act in the general interest--and also for himself. Some of the Chowchillas called it a "Savage War."

Runners now brought news to Tenaya regularly of rapidly developing events. Savage and a large group of men had attacked the Chowchillas and the others, killing many and driving them back into the foothill country beyond Coarse Gold. Though Kieyou himself led the defense, and tried personally to kill Savage, the man escaped. But from that moment on, all knew that James Savage's time was running out with The People.

Early in 1851 a Battalion of fighters was formed in Mariposa, Tenaya learned, and Savage was elected Major. From the start, it was clear that the Major would have a leading part in doing the business with the Indians. He it was who was consulted about the habits of The People, their tongues, how well they fought, which ones were to be feared, which easy prey. He knew some of the country well, the lower country.

When some of the Battalion were killed and scalped, including the ears, it was Savage who was able to explain the meaning of the practice of taking the enemies strength. Such a measure was extreme, he said, and meant one thing: the Indians were wholly committed to a battle plan and would not now come out peacefully.

Tenaya remembered the account he heard of how the white men had scalped The People in Sonoma, with no reason....

The Mariposa Battalion, it was known, had three companies of men who were determined to accomplish their task. In March, the campaign was begun.

All of this and more was reported to Tenaya within days, sometimes hours, of its occurrence. He dared not move his beloved Yosemitees down from the wintry valley now.

What should he do? If he did nothing--send no men to Kieyou--or not go down, would that be better than flight? How would they be treated by The Invaders if they gave resistance, and then went down? Would the Yosemitees be treated worse, now that Major Savage had so much military power? Would he take revenge on the Yosemitees for the murders he thought they had committed?

Day and night, though, and moment to moment his great concern was for his People. Not for a vague chance of some future, strong tribe covering the lower Sierra region, not for a superior future village of Yosemitees. His was an intense and profound concern for the individual--for Latta's daughter and wife, for Latta the steady one. He cared for jolly Seethkil, who yesterday, in the midst of troubled times, spent precious energy to climb to the Red Fir Forest to bring down some balsam oil from the young trees for an old woman who could no longer

47

walk, and could only sit and toss sticks onto her little fire. He thought of Loiya and wept....

That night at sundown, Tenaya prepared to speak to his People, directly and simply. He called them to him, even the youngest children, and when they were seated near the fires in the caves, he spoke with them.

All of them knew how trying the problems had been. All knew that Tenaya himself must act, and that his action would be done about matters he could not say that he completely understood.

The Chief looked into the open face of Loiya, who dropped her eyes to the fire, into the eager eyes of Seethkil, of Latta's sweet girl seated next to Loiya. There were well over one hundred persons in all crowding as near as possible.

Tenaya spoke briefly of the start of the war, of armed conflict. He did not dwell on details or arguments, for all knew all too well the alternatives. Which had he chosen? They were ready to accept once more his leadership as they had so often over the years.

Tenaya mentioned the ancient ones who first lived in Ahwahnee, the wise one who urged him to gather Ahwahneechees to return to their home. Grizzly was remembered--and the little dog.

The Chief was silent for a long, long time. No one stirred. Pine knots snapped in the fires and yellow flames played shadow games on the grey rock ceiling.

He would not ask the Ahwahneechees to go down. There was visible relief on many a face. He would not ask them to stay. Some showed puzzle. A new blackness, a new destruction threatens the Ahwahneechees. Once more, they must disband and seek asylum in other villages. Once more they must await the time of return to their well-loved land. Some would return to the east, some to the north. Some of the young men would want to fight, and Tenaya would not stop them. Some would remain to live the days through into sleep for as long as they were able.... He looked carefully about him once more, at The People before him, raised his head high as he stood up, and instead of wailing or chanting, he silently walked from the cave out into the moonlit, snowy night.

Latta went at once to join in the fight, was wounded in his foot within three days, and returned to recuperate. Seethkil and Till remained, at Tenaya's request, along with about forty others who were near and remote relatives of the old chief.

Sorrowfully and reluctantly, a good many of the younger adults and youths started on their journeys to villages north, south, and east. No one went west. There were few words. There were tears.

The next day the Pohonochees' older ones and children returned to the village at Pohono Creek. Tenaya ordered preparations for a winter flight to the east.

Chapter XII
The Invaders in The Valley

Seethkil, who had gone up to Wawona to speak with some of the younger Pohonochees, brought the news that the Mariposa Battalion had started from below Agua Fria, and were riding toward Chowchilla Mountain to bring back villages of Pohonochees and Yosemitees. One of The People was guiding them.

Within two days a runner came to the Caves from Wawona. He was sent by the troops under Major Savage. The message was expected: Come to the reservation on the Fresno. Bring your people to Wawona at once and you will be fairly treated. Do not, and be killed.

A winter crossing of the Sierra was a very risky undertaking for so many. The Chief could not ask them all to undertake it. In fairness, he again asked all to decide whether to go into the winter heights to Mono, or to the Fresno reservation. He would go to Major Savage himself and return in two days, if he could. By then they should have decided.

Alone, Tenaya went up to Wawona where he found the troops and Major Savage. Tenaya told the Major that his People were fearful of going to the great valley among some bad ones, that they required nothing in the way of help, and asked for nothing so much as to be left alone in their lives. The Major repeated his demands and threats of destruction, and said that his troops were prepared to go now to bring in the Yosemitees. Tenaya begged permission to go back to bring them himself. He was allowed to return.

He learned that the Pohonochees' young men had agreed to return, and that their old ones and children were

50

coming in.

About seventy-five of the Yosemitees chose to go to the reservation with Tenaya. Some forty of the family chose to start out for the east side, agreeing with Tenaya to stop at Lake Pyweack until they could hear from him. Loiya, Latta, Till, and Seethkil were among these.

Tenaya, again alone, went ahead to tell the Major of their coming. A storm delayed their trip down but all arrived safely at Wawona. Major Savage did not believe that they had all come, as indeed they had not. Tenaya explained, accurately, that some had returned to the Paiutes and Monos in the east, and others had returned to other villages and only some ancient ones were left who could not travel. Quite naturally, he said nothing about his family.

The Major refused to accept this. Forming three companies, he started out through the deep snows for Ahwah-nee, sending troops on with Tenaya and his People to start for the Fresno. It was thus that The Invaders came to Ahwahnee.

All they found was an ancient woman, sitting by her small fire in the Cave, tossing on pieces, occasionally sniffing a stick soaked in balsam oil. She ignored the soldiers.

The troops burned all acorn and other food storage, explored for other signs of the Yosemitees, and, finding none, returned to the Fresno where they learned that Tenaya and all the Yosemitees had escaped the guards and returned to the mountains. Chowchillas had frightened all by reporting that they would all be killed. Immediate reassurances of safety brought most of them back to the reservation. Even Tenaya stayed for a few hours, long enough to become sick at the sight of degeneracy of The People, at their childlike actions, and at their utter failure to realize their own imminent destruction. It was a resolute Tenaya who returned to Ahwahnee and to his family, possibly for the last time.

Chapter XIII
Spring in Ahwahnee

Tenaya was sure that the troops would come again to Ahwahnee when they had a chance, and that there was no escaping the inevitable descent to the ugly reservation with all its restrictions and threats to their well being. No wild creature wants to be constrained and forced against its nature, once it has experienced freedom.

Spring in Ahwahnee made its own demands. Robin arrived. Tenaya saw him and remembered that Robin would be the first to nest in Tuolumne Meadows, and usually brought off two broods of young in a long season. Marmot, the large golden ground squirrel, now emerged for longer and longer periods each day, keeping to warmer places and consuming any green grass it found. Black Bear who does not hibernate but does become almost torpid for long periods, came out ravenous in the early spring, and made a nuisance of himself about the village stealing anything to eat he could find, day and night.

With warming, longer days and some rains, the streams ran full and happy, if somewhat roiled. River filled each afternoon as snows and ice melted and dropped in level as night came on and lengthening shadows brought freezing temperatures to its sources in tiny rivulets and smaller streams up the slope. At Tuolumne Meadows, Mouse died by the thousands on the meadows that were flooded by the daily rising tide. Renewed life in spring was not universal. Some wildness died that other life might increase. Pine Drops and Snow Flower could not grow except in dead matter.

Pink Azelia and white as well were in full display

together now at the turn in the river by El Capitan, and would be soon at the top of the fall in Pyweack Canyon. White Dogwood tree blossoms now showed their innocent, white faces to all alike--Rattlesnake, Deer, and The People.

Deer now ran together, bucks and does and yearlings. Very soon, though, they would part, the does would separate and seek seclusion for bearing the fawn, while the bucks would flock together and find spring and summer range far up the slopes--right up to the top of the Sierra range.

Starting in Ahwahnee, Tenaya could hear the exciting roar of Yosemite Falls, now at maximum boom and volume. He could only recall those other memorable sights of Illilouette, Vernal, and Nevada, and only imagine the tremendous strength and dizzying sight of the Waterwheel Falls in Tuolumne Canyon where wheels of water turn back endlessly, rising over fifty feet in the air, their water then booming on down canyon.

Even under the pale of impending events in the life of the Ahwahneechees, Tenaya was momentarily aglow with the push and cry of spring.

It was then that he learned of the birth of Seethkil's baby boy, his first child from his new young wife. Spring in Ahwahnee came to The People, too.

Tenaya looked up at Tysiack. The afternoon warmth had melted pockets of snow on her face and she was crying.

A week later Captain Boling and his troops did arrive in the valley for a second time.

Tenaya was ready, though he did not mean to fight. He understood the force of the enemy and respected it. He had arranged for Latta, Till and Seethkil, and two others to watch the moves of the troops. Their safety lay in stealth, intelligence and retreat, They watched. The women and children had already been sent up the cliffs on their way to Pyweak Lake to wait. Tenaya and a handful of other men had stationed themselves up the steep slope of Pyweak Canyon with a quantity of rocks to defend themselves.

Latta and the others stayed on the north side of the river and watched. In plain view, making no effort to hide, they felt secure from capture because the river was high and swift. To their alarm, however, one, and then another horseman crossed with difficulty and chased them to an unfavorable position for hiding where they were captured and brought into the troop encampment.

From his eagle perch high up on the cliff, Tenaya saw three soldiers exploring the canyon, saw one climbing up. Below him, too soon, a young man, excited and inexperienced in defense, loosed rock. It carried one man down, but the other turned up and fired, killing the boy. He then descended and left with his injured companion. Tenaya was concerned that Latta or Till had not come to report.

The next morning, after a very cold night spent on the cliff, one of the young men from the camp came to Tenaya, told of his son's capture and asked him to come in. Tenaya started down the cliff to go to the camp. Before he had reached the bottom Latta ran up breathlessly. He had escaped by engaging in target shooting with the guards, had shot his arrows farther and farther behind the target, until he could safely break and run. Yes, the others were unharmed and were anxious for Tenaya's return. Tenaya sent Latta to Pyweack Lake, along with the men on the cliff, and walked rapidly past the lake of reflections. A late afternoon turbulence made the surface angry.

Chapter XIV
Indignity and Assault

Now moving more from need and instinct than from desire and choice, Tenaya walked slowly and mechanically to the troop camp in the meadow opposite the base of Yosemite Falls. The Steller Jays were complaining to each other raucously in the trees. Gray squirrel, patting his paw on the branch under him, was barking and coughing his own annoyance high in a Sugar Pine, with its huge cones pendant on the end of the upper branches. A gun shot in the distance was loud enough to make Chickaree, the lively Red Squirrel interrupt his playful feeding long enough to chatter a warning to all. Dark clouds were forming over the upper valley beyond Nevada Fall.

As he entered the meadow there was a small group of the men standing and talking and watching something in the grass. Tenaya approached them. Looking down in the grass he saw and then couldn't see what held their attention. Seethkil's body lay face down, his long black hair spread out to one side, lying over his right arm that still seemed to be raised as though he were running for his life. A gaping red hole in his back, through which still seeped the joy of his being, left no doubt of the cause.

With a wail that became a groan, Tenaya prostrated himself onto his youngest son's body, sobbing uncontrollably. The men left them there and went back to the camp not far off to wait.

After an hour or so Tenaya was aware that someone was speaking to him. It was a young Pohonochee the captain used as interpreter and guide. The boy said that Dr. Bunnell wanted to explain how this terrible accident had happened, and to assure the Chief that it was in no way the responsibility of the command, and that Captain Boling was deeply regretful.

The guard who had watched the four captive men wanted to be rid of his burden. He had been trained to believe that the only good Indian is a dead one. As a kind of morbid game, he had allowed Seethkil and Till to untie each other. They were then urged to run with a chance to escape unharmed, or to be shot in the attempt. But they had no real choice. Till and Seethkil both broke away with a desperate burst of speed through the grass, Till taking a twisting path, Seethkil a direct one. Just before Seethkil reached the edge of the meadow, the guard's gun spoke once, a red flower bloomed on his brown, muscular back, and he arched through space to his resting place without a cry.

The lad continued. The guard was being disciplined and punished for dereliction of duty and misconduct and was being sent down. Part of this Tenaya heard, for his thoughts were elsewhere. When the boy had finished, Tenaya asked the doctor if he could be allowed to cremate the body and take care of his son in the customary manner of the Ahwahnee-chees. The doctor said he would have to speak with Captain Boling. He went off, returning a short while later to report that the Captain could not grant permission and had already ordered burial in a pit nearby which was even now being dug.

Chapter XV
The Descent from Above

Tenaya was distraught and in anguish and longed to be with his family. The Captain was deaf to his requests to go out to the mountains to them, and to his insistent demand that the troops leave and let his people be at peace in their home.

Broken in spirit, Tenaya made two feeble attempts to escape, was caught at once both times. After the second attempt, when he had been reduced to an animal status by being led around on a rope, he asked to speak to the Captain. When in his presence, he gave voluble expression to his pent up feelings and most earnest desires. As though it were a final effort, he summoned great eloquence as in earlier times. To all who had been insensitive to his internal turmoil and anguish, and who had interpreted his impassive exterior show as evidence of his not being disturbed, his brief speech came as a surprise.

In a full, rich, baritone voice he asked the Captain to kill him, as they had killed his Seethkil, letting him run, and then shooting him in the back, with no way to defend himself. Then the Captain would have the dear land of Ahwahnee free of its rightful possessors: The People who knew and loved it. Destroy all of The People, he said, for that seems to be your wish. With your guns, your horses and your many men, you can take whatever you want and The People cannot stop you. All The People will die. When he died, he promised, his spirit would make trouble for the Captain, his Great Father government and all of their people, You may destroy him, he said, but you cannot destroy the spirit of the old chief and his

Ahwahneechees. They will return to Ahwahnee. Their spirits will be in the rocks, the waterfalls, the trees, animals and in the very pohonos, cool winds that blow across the land. Their spirits will float on gentle snowflake, and drive in cold blasts of ice crystals. You may kill us, but our spirits will not leave our home. Our spirits will follow in your footsteps. Wherever you may go, we will be with you there.

For answer, Captain Boling ordered Dr. Bunnell and a few others to explore the region about Hummo Canyon at once to try to find the remainder of the Yosemitees. Tenaya, still tied, was taken along, but not as guide, nor were his infrequent comments given any weight in their decisions, for they no longer trusted him in the least to give them the truth about his People's location.

And so it happened that the small party ascended to Mt. Hoffman by way of Hummo Canyon past the Lost Arrow, and by forced march, made a circle around and back to the region above the waters of reflection by late evening. Anxious to return to camp that night, Dr. Bunnell finally consented to Tenaya's suggested route down the face of the cliff, at times necessitating removing their shoes for safety. In the last dim light of alpenglow, Dr. Bunnell confessed that he could not see any way down, when Tenaya walked over and into the top of a great oak tree, and thus descended the final few feet to safety.

Chapter XVI
The Battle at Lake Pyweack

Though it was late in May, the snow lay deep at the base of Mt. Hoffman and the nights were snapping cold. At Pyweack Lake, Loiya, Latta and the others were trying to be patient. Learning nothing they were alarmed and concerned both for Tenaya and themselves.

Seethkil's baby was getting his daily ice bath in the lake and was the object of everyone's special care. He never lacked for protectors.

Without the thick, heavy cedar bark of lower elevations, they fashioned their wickiups by weaving the resilient boughs of Hemlock around Lodgepole Pine frames, and then covering the entire fabric with other materials leaning against it. In this way they stayed fairly comfortable. The Red Fir bark, plentiful there, made fine coals for small fires.

Spring comes late in the year at the higher elevations. Loiya did notice that Robin was nesting, and that Hemlock was springing up here and there during the middle of the day, as the snow released its wintry grip on the tree.

Latta and others had made frequent trips to the edge of Ahwahnee but had learned very little to relate. Food was not plentiful. They missed the acorn meal. Hunters brought in snared Grouse from behind Pyweack Peak on the back, sunny slope where Grouse spends the entire winter. They shot Snowshoe Hare, now white, and collected the end growth of the Whitebark Pine. With what they had been able to carry they were not starving. Still, the waiting was trying. Loiya often wondered whether or not to go on over to the Monos. She let the thought perish in her mind, remembering Tenaya's resolute desire to remain as long as possible.

Loiya was a marvel with the children, teaching them the ways of Winter unceasingly--why the snow melts around the base of the Lodgepole, how to tell the height of snow in Summer by the color of the boles of the trees, and why the Lodgepole is twisted, some in one way, some in another. She taught them how to be warm in a snow cave.

She told all of the old legends, over and over again, as children and adults wish. She told of the First People Animals, and how they became animals, of the formation of the world, of the last great resting place of Elowin. She told of Hummo, of how the young hunter, Leemee was to signal to his bride, Teeheenay, from the cliff top how much game to be ready for in celebrating the wedding feast, of how he fell over and was killed, and of how his sweet bride herself was lowered to the base of Lost Arrow on sinew ropes to bring up his broken body; of how she died of her exertions at the top and went with him to Elowin, leaving the Lost Arrow as a monument to their great, unfulfilled love. Few eyes were dry when she finished, no matter how many times they had heard it.

A favorite one was called The Woman Who Was Not Satisfied.

Once near the wet frame of the world in the West, Loiya began, a tired man and his wife stopped traveling to spend the night in a cave. The man placed his buckeye fire-stick between his hands and begin spinning it on top of a dry piece of pine. The cheerful fire in the cave warmed them.

The wife and husband were hungry after their long journey. Hutulu, the Great Horned Owl, hooted from the shadowy top of a Ponderosa Pine near them. The wife asked the husband to call the owl, as he was skilled at making the sound and drawing the great bird close for a kill. The husband was a skilled hunter. He could get closer than all others to deer with his deer-skin and antlers cloak over him.

The husband nocked an arrow and called slowly, hutulu, hutulu, hutulu. (Loiya, too, was skilled at making bird sounds).

The owl answered. Husband called. Owl came closer and called. When the bird was near the fire the husband shot and killed it. The wife and husband ate it hungrily.

Wife asked him to call again so that they might eat another. Husband called hutulu, hutulu, hutulu. Another owl came and he shot it.

The wife wanted more owls to eat. She said they were very hungry, had eaten little meat for days of journeying, that they needed meat tomorrow in the daytime when the owls are gone.

The husband nocked another arrow and called once more. Two owls came immediately, followed by five of the great birds. Silent as owls are in flight, so many came that there was a roar of rustling feathers and ear pounding sound of the hooting of the cloud of owls in the cave, their wings fanning the fire to great brightness.

Husband shot all of his arrows. Still the owls flocked through the entrance of the cave. Husband placed his wife under a large basket for protection, seized burning brands from the fire to hurl at Hutulu.

Suddenly the owls descended on the man and the woman, killing them both, thus achieving revenge for the selfish and needless killing of the Hutulu.

Loiya told of the time their Chief Tenaya killed the Grizzly and named his People. Loiya remembered the details. And Loiya remembered Kisskisska Meadows....

Latta brought the word in the night that the troops had come up Pyweack Canyon and were heading for Pyweack Lake, that Tenaya was with them tied to a rope, and that Till had been captured again, having ventured too close. It was Loiya who decided, more to relieve Latta of embarrassment than to take the command from the man. She asked Latta to tell The People to gather their materials for a camp, and to wait quietly for the soldiers to find them. No one was to leave, and no one was to do any violent act.

In the early sun of morning Loiya, with Latta's small daughter Wadacka by her side, and with an arm around the shoulders of Seethkil's widow, her hair cut short in mourning, faced and met the soldiers with quiet dignity.

The soldiers made much of the capture, as though it were difficult to walk around women and children, and greatly exaggerated their deeds. Loiya was disgusted to hear later how they spoke of the affair. Pyweack Lake was frozen over so solidly that a man could walk out on it. The wickiups still had smoke curling from their tops when the strange procession started for the Ahwahnee, perhaps for the last time. Still unwilling, they were at last resigned. Tenaya, after family greetings, fell silent again. Ky, limping still, was the last to follow.

Chapter XVII
Capture and Resignation

The distance from Pyweack Lake to Ahwahnee, thence by Wawona to the Fresno plain and San Joaquin Valley is about a three day's journey for a strong man on foot. With children, and burdened with their household goods and treasures, the trip was a difficult one under forced march. The troops, elated with their success which signaled the end of the war, were eager to get back to their post to enjoy a celebration, leaves, and possibly mustering out. The Yosemites and Tenaya, of all the Indians, were the very last ones to come in. Their eagerness did little to slow them for the Ahwahneechees' comfort. Indeed they were impatient with Tenaya and the others for being so slow. Some of the troops finally went on ahead, as they drew near the reservation.

The children were excited by the novelty and the anticipation, but the adults were extremely apprehensive. The weather did its share to kill their spirits, for it was one of those blistering hot, dry days of early June, when the thermometer itself becomes a heater, that greeted them. The contrast between their camp at Pyweack Lake and the cauldron at the reservation could not have been greater.

Good weather would have done little to reassure them. Within an hour on the reservation they learned all they needed to know and had expected from reports.

The shacks that had been hastily erected for them were improperly equipped, were over-crowded, and were terrible in the heat. Toilet facilities, installed for "sanitation" merely concentrated the sources of filth and disease in a manner the Yosemites would never permit in the wild. Regulations for

65

clothing were ruinous. Women, accustomed to little, were bundled up for "decency" and were over-heated. Men who had run nude, but not naked, chafed under the burden of garments that were at best cheap and ill-fitting. They even looked ugly, like children dressed up to be adults playing "house."

Villages that had been conveniently separated in the mountains were within easy walks of each other. Suspicions of disloyalties among husbands and wives, bickering among the contentious, and hostile fights were common. Fairly jostling one another by comparison and building from mountain grown animosities of long years' standing, The People were miserable. No one was free from the troubles.

New diseases broke out. Pneumonia had killed a good many the past winter, and strange new sores developed here and there on the reservation that some said came from the miners themselves and could kill in a long time. There were rumors that violent revenge would come.

The People had been promised payment for their territories as compensation for the loss. Besides getting a "share" of the reservation, clothing, shelter, and food, they were due money for their property. Few even heard about that on the reservation. Some vaguely explained that the Great Father failed to grant the money for payments. What the father grants, they thought, the father can take away.

Tenaya, agitated and restive even before arriving was in a terrible state within days. The last to be brought in with the last People to give in, instead of being admired by the others they were the objects of ridicule and scorn. Tenaya smarted. He was disgusted with all he saw. He scoffed at talk of payment. What was Ahwahnee worth? To the Ahwahnee-chees? He was contemptuous of the very question. One does not price what has true value.

At each opportunity, Tenaya went to the authority asking that the Yosemitees be allowed to return, that he be allowed to go for awhile, because they did not like the food, it was bad for them, they could not care for their children who were becoming uncontrollable. They longed for acorns that did not grow in the heated valley, it was too hot for them who were used to the mountains, they were being pestered and teased by bad Indians and were growing sick.

To be rid of the annoyance, Tenaya and his immediate family were permitted to return to Ahwahnee on condition of good behavior and that they should not consider it as theirs or as a home ever again.

Like released prisoners, Tenaya and his small family band walked up out of the furnace into their Eden once more. Never before had the sweathouse been so refreshing, the river so friendly. Never before had the acorn been more flavorful, the onion so plentiful. Never before had the music of the falls sounded so sweet. For a moment, there was joy in the happy return. Even though there was no answer to the question in all their minds, there had come to be less necessity to try to answer. Events, not thoughts, would provide the answer. Still it would not down. How long?

Chapter XVIII
Promises and Defaults

The People on the eastern side had not been brought in, and had escaped the harsh armed treatment of those on the western slope of the Sierra. The Monos were among those few to be free of the travail--for awhile.

Kuna heard the reports but saw that there was little the Monos could do without endangering themselves. He sent word of welcome to any who wished to come. Beyond that he could only sympathize, Kuna heard how the word of the Great Government far away had turned sour, of Tenaya's return, and of the small band of Pohonochees who went back to Pohono Creek Village.

He and others began to speak of their own territory and its future. So far they had lived peaceably enough with Miners in Bodie, Bennettville and elsewhere. For how long? The question would not be answered. Would the troops simply drive out the Monos, too?

Kuna was only partly surprised to see the band of Ahwahneechees walking toward him with Tenaya leading. But he was frightened at Tenaya's story of why they had come.

A group of miners had come to Ahwahnee to prospect for gold. At Pohono Creek two were killed, the others returning to Coarse Gold to report that the Yosemitees had murdered the men. The truth was, Tenaya said, that one of the men, hoping to jump the claims of the others in Coarse Gold, had arranged ahead of time for some Pohono young men, not Yosemitees, to ambush the party and to stop them and to help kill the other men. No one knows what to say with an easy tongue beyond that. Other murders and ransackings had been blamed on The

69

People that were done by the miners and ranchers themselves--including stealing horses. Tenaya told of the most infamous thief who wore horseshoes on a board so as to escape detection and succeeded very well until his trail of prints was followed over two high fences.

Tenaya continued. Three men went out to prospect with the others remaining in camp to prepare food. Two returned running, screaming that they should run and hide or all be killed by the Indians. They were wounded by arrows. They retreated from the Valley and took the word to the troops who came into the Valley, found five young Pohonochees whom they called Yosemitees with the clothing of the dead men, lined them up and shot them.

Fearing for their lives, Tenaya and his family had fled to the Monos.

Kuna listened carefully to this account. He believed the old chief. He told Tenaya that they were welcome to stay with the Monos as long as they wished. If they needed food, it would be brought. Their presence would be concealed by the Monos. The two old chiefs found great comfort in each other and in their long friendship.

Chapter XIX
Tenaya's Hegira

Tenaya and his family remained safely hidden from the troops during the winter of 1851-1852 with the Monos. Feeling that enough time had elapsed since the attack on the miners in the valley so that they could return unnoticed, Tenaya announced their intentions to Kuna. Ahwahnee still pulled powerfully.

Before departing, the old friends played the hand gambling game one night. It was now well into summer, and the Mono Lake night was dry and warm. The air was heady with the vanilla-pineapple scent of the Jeffrey Pine, the Sage bloomed, the hunters had brought in the first Mountain Sheep for a special feast, and all spirits were raised. Tenaya and his family had been well treated, and though they were pleased with their stay with the Monos, their love for Ahwahnee and its ways was overpowering.

The game was a rousing one. Even Tenaya took more open chances than he ordinarily would have, for he was exuberant over the prospects of returning across the Sierra. At one point when the scorekeeper held all but one counter in favor of the Yosemitees, he sang spontaneously and loudly, a rare display for him. Kuna as usual was boisterous and made a number of humorous jibes at the expense of his guests. He call the Yosemitees The Beaten Grizzlies. He taunted some about the western people in general with their humiliating defeats at the hands of the ignorant, soft whites with their horses and guns.

The women watched that night and the children made some side bets early in the evening. Loiya left the gay circle early, though, and in the company of Seethkil's widow walked part way up the slope of the large, volcanic cinder cone nearest the lake. It was moonlight, still and warm, and the snow patches up under the tops of the sharp crest of the escarpment of the Sierra reflected the glory. At night the darkness of the mountains was exaggerated. So too was the bright whiteness. Across the silence from the village she could hear the game in progress, could even make out Tenaya's strong voice raised in song once more.

During the evening one of Kuna's hunters told the group of a plan to go get horses from a large cattle rancheria south of them in the San Joaquin Valley over the Sierra. Being so far away, they would not be suspected. At this time of year the animals would be best to eat, for they would have fed on the spring pastures but would not have been worked hard so early in the season. The very thought of roasted pieces of horse flesh roused their appetites, especially those of the young men who never seem to be satisfied in food or activity. Like Chickaree, the small dark-red squirrel, young men take exercise on every possible occasion and seem to take energy from exertion.

The young Mono asked if any of Tenaya's young men would like to accompany them to bring back horses. Each man meant at least one more horse. Tenaya did not notice how the young men answered. He was absorbed in the game and in his thoughts of the return......

The small band left their hosts early in the morning two days later. Loiya, Latta and his two wives, Seethkil's robust son, completely exposed to the goodness of summer, the boy's mother, Till and his three wives and six children who trotted along with a few other youngsters of varying ages, and eleven others, including two ancient ones, women, made up the entire group. By contrast with the very large village of Monos who watched them leave for Red Rock Canyon (called Bloody Canyon by the miners), theirs was a pitiful group.

As they walked slowly up the canyon, Latta recalled his winter trek and the white deer, and while they rested at one of the lakes just below the pass itself, he told the story twice, for when he had finished it the first time the children clamored to hear it again. Sitting there and looking at the very red wall where he had actually had the vision made an indelible image on all.

As he finished speaking Latta looked up and saw clouds beginning to form over Koip Peak and Kuna Crest. At this elevation, high above Mono basin at the crest of the Sierra, these clouds, wispy on the edges, filtered sunlight and became crystals of light such as the quartz Latta and Seethkil had found on the tableland of Echo Peaks, pure white, glassy pieces with flat surfaces as broad as a woman's hand, weighing as much as a child. They had brought back some of the smaller ones as treasures, he remembered.

The clouds this early in the day promised rain by afternoon. The band, still moving slowly down from the pass, arrived at the Tuolumne River just before the rain began late in the afternoon. The summer thunderstorm was violent and passed rapidly. The skies cleared before sundown. Freshness in the air and a few signs were all they now felt of the passing turbulence, signs such as dead pine cones that had closed up tightly again after getting wet and rolling under foot, or the string of round water mirrors leading off among the trees caused by Black Bear who always takes the same trail and places his feet in the same spots, making cupped depressions. Even the young bear hops along dutifully using the established trail, up over snow banks earlier in the season, and then, as the bank disappears, following the same treading spots down onto the forest duff.

After the storm the birds became active, feeding hungrily during the short period before dark. The fiery Sierra Crossbill with its twisted beak for breaking open the scales of green pine cones was overhead dropping scales down on the band. Up on the slopes of the dominating dome near the river they could hear the familiar brack-bracking of Clark Crows, and could see their grey forms here and there as they came flying down in sweeping, undulating paths. The Yosemitees had counted five, not three, calls of the Chickadee birds as they cheerfully flitted from branch tip to branch tip.

At Pyweack Lake the next day Tenaya, on a sudden desire, left the group, saying that he wanted to go on alone by a different route for the remainder of the trip and that he would meet them at the Caves in Ahwahnee. By setting up their tiny village at the Caves they would be less noticed by any visitors who might venture up. Latta took them down the short way in Pyweack Canyon that would go past the waters of reflection to the Caves. Tenaya left them at the outlet of the lake, where the remnant had been captured a few months ago, and started across the canyon top behind Pyweack Peak. Dr. Bunnell had remarked to him, he recalled, that the troops named the lake Tenaya. He had simply scorned the gesture, for it had the name Pyweack, meaning shining rocks, for many lives. People might sensibly be named for places--Ahwahneechees--or for animals--Yosemitees--but not places for people. He scoffed again just remembering.

Tenaya walked rapidly after ascending the first steep ridge, passed ponds alive with frogs and through small meadows strewn with flowers. He noticed that Sierra Shooting Star was at the height of its season. Each growing thing, he thought, has its own conditions of life, its season, and then passes. Gravel Garlic won't grow in the meadow dampness, Shooting Stars in the dry gravel. Deer browse the outside leaves of ceanothus bushes, Porcupine eats the bark of young trees and bushes. And the Ahwahneechees' season......?

Leaving the damp meadows he went up into drier slopes of crumbling granite, through an open, climax forest of Jeffrey Pine, some Juniper, and, Red Fir, and came eventually to the summit of Cloud's Rest, his intended objective.

It had been a long time since he had troubled to climb to such a prominence. He could not have picked a better moment. Sun was dropping in the west, toward Elowin, here and there a few clouds hung over his familiar mountains. From

74

here he could look back and see small snow patches showing peaks they had just journeyed around and through and could see much more. To the south there was range on range that seemed to get higher and higher as the eye followed their progression. They even seemed to be moving, for shadows were fast falling. Nearer to him, the Red Peak and the Black Peak were in deep color. To the north the breathtaking drop into Pyweack Canyon stopped his eye short, then released it to the relief of watching the sharper tops of the range in Tuolumne.

Finally he turned last of all and looked down past Tysiack's mass straight into the heart of Ahwahnee and he was glad. The toy forests of Ahwahnee were already in the dark and the river, snaking its way down the valley, could barely be made out. As he beheld the loved sight his vision dimmed and became liquid....

Anxious to be there now that he had at last seen it he went straight in line toward Tysiack's back, down the side of the summit of Cloud's Rest, dropping from there to the river, and passed the falls in moonlight. He fairly ran to the Caves.

The next day his family arrived, as delighted as he to be home once more amid the familiar surroundings, deep in the memories of the past life of the Ahwahneechees, close to the spirits of those gone before. All of his family had arrived.

The next morning two young men went to visit the Pohonochees' village and failed to return that night or the next or for a long time. No one knew where they were. Since this was not unusual for young men to visit neighboring villages to meet young women, it was not thought to be serious. Still, with so few hunters now it placed an additional burden on the others to bring in enough game. Their provisions were very low, the acorn crop had been small the previous year, the Band Tailed Pigeons were scarce for some unexplained reason, and Tenaya was concerned why they had not stayed for a few days before leaving. He understood though how strong the summer urges a man, especially a young man. He understood how the months of separation from the young girl friends peaked their curiosity to see them, to talk with them, to be near them. He understood......

Chapter XX
The Game of Death

Ribbon and Pigeon Falls had both dried up and the river had dropped before the two young hunters returned bringing a horse with them. It was a small yearling. Even then it was more than they could all eat in two or three days and so some of it was stripped and hung in the summer sun to dry against a day of future need. The remainder was eaten and the bones tossed aside as pleasant reminders of their feast, a kind of homecoming thanksgiving. The hunters explained to Tenaya that they had found the horse wandering in the forest on Big Creek near Wawona.

Tenaya knew of such escapades of youth in his village from time to time. Since he placed so little value on the horse except as food he didn't trouble himself with the morals of stolen meat thirty miles distant across the mountain. The horse was of no other use to him. Where and why should he ride? Many of the places he needed to go were impossible for a horse to walk in without breaking a leg or falling over. Moreover, they wanted to eat the best grasses and clovers that The People preferred. With the meat still in short supply, the animal was a welcome gift. He did not trouble to pry about what else the young men had done. It was the warm season and high blood runs strong.

Not until a year later did Loiya learn the full account. Three more horses were being held for them, one back in Wawona, and two at the Pohono village down the valley. All of the animals came from the cattle rancheria far south and were caught by the hunters in company with the Pohonochees and six young Monos. The hunters were to take only one for

77

each hunter, as they had agreed. The two Yosemitees took four. They had returned by a long route but their trail had been followed. The Monos knew who had taken their prizes.

Mono drums began to sound softly in their dwellings soon after the discovery. On the third night dancing and chanting had begun. Kuna knew what he had to do.

No runners came to warn Tenaya of the Monos' coming. The village was too small for a regular watch. There would have been no cause for alarm in any event for the first Monos, the only ones they saw, numbered only eight, Kuna, two older men and five young carriers with obsidian, pine nuts and kachavee.

Tenaya greeted the visitors warmly in the afternoon. He wondered for a moment why they had come so soon after his band's leaving. He assumed that Kuna would be trading farther down with other villages. He was more alarmed that all the men showed the signs of having taken the drug of tanyuwish plant roots. When Kuna proposed the hand game after sundown, Tenaya understood, for tanyuwish was often taken in secret by players to give them the advantage of detecting opponents' intentions by heightened powers. Like the drunkard who thinks his unsteadiness is undetected, tanyuwish users gave themselves away. Some used it before going into battle....

Kuna was reluctant to accept his hunters' stories until he saw the bones and the drying horse flesh. With the certainty born of ignorance of the total facts, he was no longer in doubt. He was determined to go ahead with the plan.

The game started with Tenaya passing the bones beneath the rabbit skin blanket to Latta, Latta to Till, then back again to Tenaya who passed one of them on to an old one next to him. Kuna began to chant in loud tones with a raucous, forced voice. He has taken additional tanyuwish, thought Tenaya. The scorekeeper was an older Mono. Kuna and the three others watched the Yosemitees very intently and quietly. The game, thought Kuna, is going well. Kuna was winning.

Loiya watched from the shadows. Later after the

children left for sleep and the old ones lost interest, she watched.

The moon went up over Tysiack so bright you could see tear stains, now dry tears in the middle of summer. The moon passed beyond Lost Arrow and sailed off behind towering, black clouds flashing lightning, leaving the Caves in deep shadow.

The second time Coyote barked Tenaya listened. He thought it strange that Valley Coyote was in Ahwahnee, instead of Mt. Coyote. Wise in the ways of nature he was not certain that it should be strange and so ignored it. The third time the barking was closer.

Kuna had stopped singing entirely. Kuna was quiet. Two young Monos had casually worked their way behind Tenaya. The Yosemitee hunters, still full of their horse flesh meal, slept on the ground not far away. Loiya watched from the shadows.

Kuna lay back his head. He howled a Coyote howl note and then wailed an ear piercing note. The sound of quick steps was heard. Before he could turn, Tenaya's head was crushed by a large stone. He fell back senseless and lay still on the earth. Till half rose to his feet and was struck down. Latta threw himself backwards, sprang up to meet a spear that penetrated his throat. There were no screams or shouts. It was a quiet game.

Kuna and the other players hurriedly left the circle.

Loiya watched from the shadows.

Stone was piled on stone as twenty-five Monos who had been hiding came to throw their vengeful share, until the dead and the dying were buried under the stones of Ahwahnee.

The game was ended.

Epilogue

"You cannot destroy the spirit of the old chief and his Ahwahneechees. They will return to Ahwahnee. Their spirits will be in the rocks, the waterfalls, the trees, animals, and in the pohonos. Their spirits will float on gentle snowflake, and drive in cold blasts of ice crystals. You may kill us but our spirits will not leave our home...."

Today you may hear and feel the pohono winds blowing Bridalveil Falls, veiling her waters upward on air. Seethkil's spirit abounds in red and grey squirrel's actions throughout the Sierran forests (Seethkil means 'squirrel'). Climb high up on a loosely piled talus slope and move large granite chunks, then you may hear voices magmatic, granular, and unmistakable. In the deep of a dark hemlock forest, steep, you may listen for the whispered tones of breeze speech.

At Tenaya Lake in the spring, where Seethkil's babe was bathed, the ice breaking up cracks its chatter as it warms, stirring Clark's crows to bracking. Truly the Sierra Nevada are crowded with voices of the past--speechless voices of eloquence. Ahwahneechee voices murmur on...

Still, in the spring when the snows have stopped, Tysiack cries, and hutulu quietly calls with his flute-voice from high in the towering forest.

Author's Note

While writing Tenaya's speech in the Cave on the porch of the cabin of the Carnegie Experimental Gardens at Mather I paused to look out and there, unbelievably, stood a large cinnamon-colored Black Bear with a hump much like the Grizzly's. Under the circumstances there was nothing else for me to do. I spoke to him, whereupon he turned about in a rather kittenish fashion (thus breaking the possible spell) and walked off into the deep forest.

A ready complaint about Indian stories is that the "noble savage" theme has been overdrawn and overworked. Apologists for the Indian abound. Do we need another? Well, I suspect that the reason we are impressed with the increasing number of so-called apologists is that we now know so much more of an accurate kind of what the Indian life was, and that any story that appears using precise anthropological, ethnographical, and even linguistical information is bound to give the impression of special pleading. It is my belief, though, that the extremes of both nobility and savagery can be best avoided by sticking rather closely to the facts of the matter. Indeed, the facts alone, once you get some of the detail, are fascinating. Instead of making a noble of Tenaya and the Yosemitees, or taking them as savages, I have tried to see them as simple human beings of a very distinctive kind trying simply to be human beings. What's wrong, I found myself asking, with just being a fine human being, without being a leader, a musician, a philosopher, or even a writer? Tenaya's story and that of The People throughout the land is tragic in the classical tradition. No one could have prevented the outcome of the invasion. No one could have prevented the destruction of the California Indians. Each growing thing has its season and passes....

Most of the names used in the story are authentic names used by California Indians, though not necessarily by Yosemitees. Some are fictional and invented. Latta is the name of an author who has written about the Indians. Loiya was the Indian word for the Spanish word for "pot," la olla, Seethkil meant squirrel and Till meant quail, both in Miwok.

The ethnological and geographical information, as well as the natural history information, for the most part, is accurate and authentic, though it is probably not for me to say so. Valley Coyote does occur in the Yosemite Valley and it would be passing strange if Mt. Coyote did today. Some of the information sounds wrong, like having Band Tailed Pigeons in Yosemite. They do occur there to this day but not commonly. I have seen one on the summit of Mammoth Peak in Tuolumne Meadows at 5:00 a.m. during August. White deer still occur but are very rare. The Indians actually did prize them. Who wouldn't--even the vision would be priceless, as Latta found. The use of drugs is a fact, though I have intentionally suppressed the accurate name of the very common plant used, for obvious reasons. This is not meant to be a scientific paper. It is a story.

It is sometimes necessary for a fiction writer to take liberties with the truth in an historical novel. Even historians can be downright libertine with facts. It should be said that the interpretation I make of the major events in this book are based on a careful research of basic sources and documents and that such interpretations, in each case, are defensible in an historical sense, and are plausible when the facts are missing. Whatever new information I have found has served to confirm me in my earliest suspicions that the first records of the events were highly prejudicial and in favor of the settlers, miners, traders-- The Invaders.

Major Savage may not have been the complete scoundrel depicted, I grant, and Tenaya may not have been quite so innocent of complicity against the Monos, but in both cases the evidence has not been stretched out of recognizable shape from the documents, The whole story is so sketchy that there is vast room for disagreement about interpretation. But once more, as history, the story told here is false. Any chapter will show you that. But it is all based on history. Only a very few paragraphs, for instance, on Tenaya exist.

Interpretation is unavoidable. For example, the Pohonochees were not carefully distinguished from the Yosemitees by the settlers. They lived within easy walking distance from each other on opposite sides of the river in Yosemite Valley, the Yosemitees on the "Grizzly" side, the Pohonochees on the "Coyote" side. (Now you can see why coyote is my marplot!) When the two miners were killed near Bridalveil (Pohono) Creek in 1852 the Yosemitees could easily have been entirely innocent, as they are made in the story. As another example, Tenaya could have been innocent of any knowledge of the stealing of the horses from the Monos. After all, he and his band did actually live with the Monos for over a year, were the most obvious, near, cross-Sierra village where the Monos would look. And the Monos, according to an Indian eye-witness account, did come to the valley to do the awful deeds--but not, of course, to play a game. That is my idea. For Tenaya to have made such a blunder is highly inconsistent with what we know by reputation years later about his sagacity, when his figure was still central in the annual Cry Ceremony.

There is a great deal that is entirely fictional, and I do not want now to disenchant you with explanations. A few points might be of interest though. Loiya is wholly a product of my desire. Tenaya's three sons, to a certain extent, are our three sons. Seethkil's baby just seemed a warm touch and relieved some of the grief over his murder. Latta's trip across the Sierra in winter in two days is possible but it would reach the limits of human endurance to do it.

One more fact. Tenaya's body, one account has it, was cremated and given a traditional burial. Indian burial grounds were carefully guarded secrets. One theory is that Tenaya's remains lie buried at Hite's Cove on the South Fork of the

Merced River.

Though he was not the very last chief of the Yosemitees he was the most famous and probably at least as fine a human being as I have thought it proper to depict. He may have been superior. Though we might turn down an invitation to join his village, it appears that millions of persons still answer the powerful call of Ahwahnee and hurry there on the slightest pretext to love it.

Portions of this story were published by the Montana Indian Publication Fund and distributed by the Montana Reading Publications, Billings, Montana 59101, under the title, *The Tragedy of Tenaya: Story of the Yosemite Indians*, 1974, Copyright by Allan Shields.